Almira's Violets

CLAUDIA FREGOSI

Almira's Violets

GREENWILLOW BOOKS

A Division of William Morrow & Company, Inc./New York

AFRICAN VIOLET FOOD

1 2 3 4 5 80 79 78 77 76

Library of Congress Cataloging in Publication Data
Fregosi, Claudia.   Almira's violets.
Summary: Jealous of all the attention Almira's violets
get, Almira's cat eats all the blossoms with grave but
effective results.
[1. Cats—Fiction]   I.   Title.
PZ7.F884Al   [E]   75-26996
ISBN 0-688-80028-9   ISBN 0-688-84028-0 lib. bdg.

Almira had a violet shop and a little cat
to keep her company.
Almira's violets grew the brightest blossoms,
the biggest blossoms, and the most blossoms
of any in the world.
When people were sad, they came in to look
at the violets.
"Your violets always cheer me up, Almira,"
they said.
Almira smiled. The cat rubbed against her leg.
You can't pet a violet, he thought.

Spring, summer, fall, and winter
Almira's violets blossomed.
When winter winds blew snow, the few people
that were out liked to come into the shop.
"It's always spring in your shop, Almira," they said.
Almira smiled. The cat sat in front of the violets
and washed his whiskers, thinking, I never saw
a violet that could wash itself.

Almira's Violets

The cat sniffed a violet and curled up in the window.
Almira's violets bloomed prettier than ever.

Until one morning . . .

Almira opened her shop.

There was not a blossom to be seen.

Not one bloom. Not one bud.

"What has happened?" cried Almira.

Almira's Violets

She put on her glasses
and looked at the violets.
She watered them.
She fed them medicine.
She talked to them.

She dusted their leaves.
She turned the heat up.
She turned the heat down.
She sang French love songs.

She turned on the grow lights,
and the night light, and the flashlight,
the black light, the red light,
and the ultraviolet light.
Nothing worked.
The cat jumped into her lap and purred.
"You're very happy," said Almira.
Violets can't purr, he said to himself.

People stayed away from the shop.

They stayed away when they were happy.

They stayed away when they were sad.

No one came in.

"It's no use," said Almira.

"I will have to sell the shop."

Oh, no! thought the cat, and he jumped
up and bit off a violet leaf.
"You!" cried Almira. "Why did you eat
the violets?"
The cat rubbed against her leg.
Almira thought for a minute.

"Were you hungry?" she asked.

The cat rubbed against her other leg.

"Were you lonely?"

The cat licked his paw.

"Were you jealous?"

The cat sat in her lap and purred.

Almira rushed to the door.

"Everybody," she called. "I know what
happened to my violets. The cat ate them."

Almira's Violets

"Off to the cannery to be made into dog food!"
someone shouted.
"Let the taxidermist stuff him!" yelled another.
"No good'll come from the cat till he's skinned
and made into mittens," said someone else.

"No," said Almira. "I think my cat has
the brightest eyes, the longest whiskers,
and the friendliest purr of any cat
in the world. Spring, summer, fall, winter,
he is my faithful friend."
"He is," said everyone.

From then on, when people came into
the violet shop they said, "It's no wonder
you have the prettiest violets, Almira,
with such a fine cat to watch over them."